FOR ERIC

A FEIWEL AND FRIENDS BOOK
An Imprint of Macmillan

ANOTHER BROTHER. Copyright © 2012 by Matthew Cordell. All rights reserved.
Printed in China by Toppan Leefung, Dougguan City, Guangdong Province. For information, address
Feiwel and Friends, 175 Fifth Avenue, New York, N.Y. 10010.

Library of Congress Cataloging-in-Publication Data

Cordell, Matthew,
Another brother / written and illustrated by Matthew Cordell. — 1st ed.
p. cm.
Summary: Davy the sheep wishes he had time alone with his parents, as he did before his twelve brothers came along
and started imitating his every move, but when his wish comes true Davy misses playing with the youngsters.
ISBN: 978-0-312-64324-9
[1. Brothers—Fiction. 2. Imitation—Fiction. 3. Family life—Fiction. 4. Sheep—Fiction.] I. Title.
PZ7.C815343Ano 2012
[E]—dc22
2011001135

The artwork was created with pen and ink with watercolor.

Book design by Matthew Cordell and Kathleen Breitenfeld

Feiwel and Friends logo designed by Filomena Tuosto

First Edition: 2012

10 9 8 7 6 5 4 3 2 1

mackids.com

ANOTHER BROTHER

MATTHEW CORDELL

FEIWEL AND FRIENDS • NEW YORK

For four glorious years, Davy had Mom and Dad all to himself.

When Davy sang a tender ballad, Dad cried.

When Davy knitted a woolly masterpiece, Mom rejoiced.

When Davy sheared his own dandy hairdo, Mom and Dad cried and rejoiced.

But, things change. . . .

Davy got a brother, Petey!

When Davy sang, Petey cried.

When Davy knitted, Petey spat up.

When Davy sheared, Petey "needed potty."

And if that wasn't enough . . .

Davy got another brother, Mike!
Then another brother, Stu!

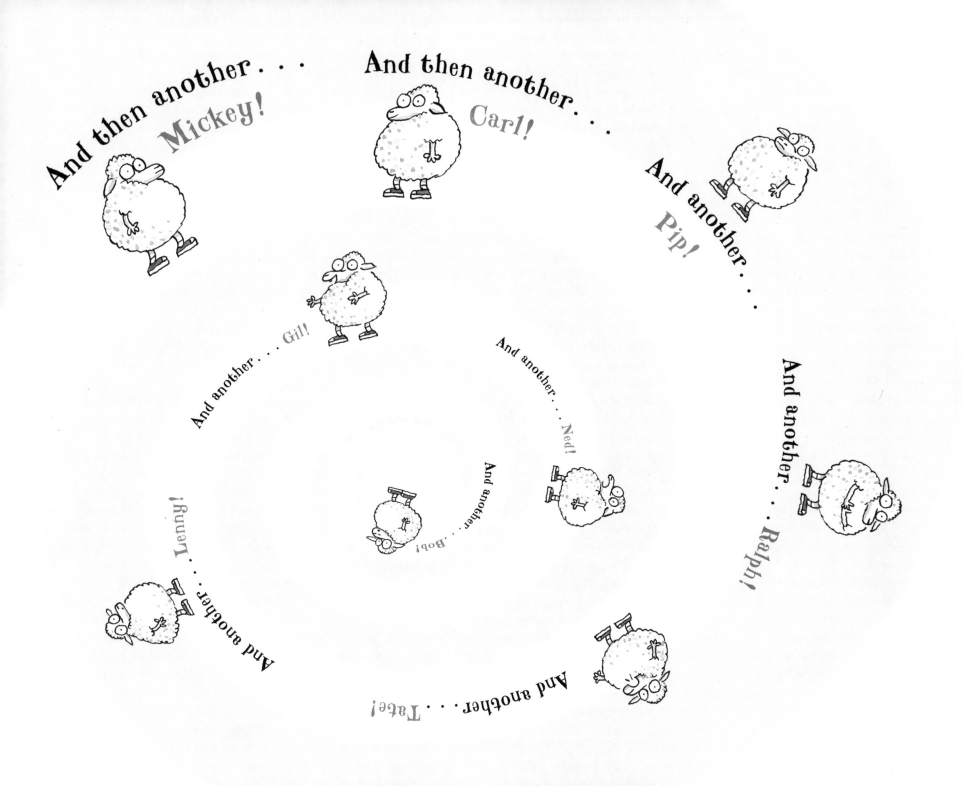

12 WHOLE BROTHERS!

Davy was just one of the bunch.

But, it got worse.

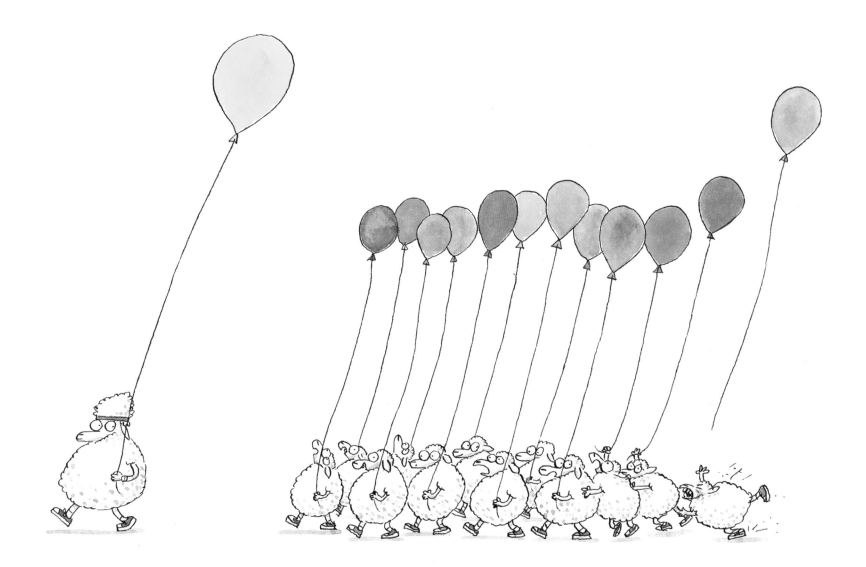

Soon, whenever Davy would do something, all twelve of his little brothers would do the exact same thing.

Davy ate Toot Loops for breakfast. Petey, Mike, Stu, Mickey, Carl, Pip, Ralph, Tate, Lenny, Gil, Ned, and Bob ate Toot Loops, too.

Davy walked around like a monkey. Petey, Mike, Stu, Mickey, Carl, Pip, Ralph, Tate, Lenny, Gil, Ned, and Bob walked around like monkeys, too.

Davy ran away—as fast as he could! Petey, Mike, Stu, Mickey, Carl, Pip, Ralph, Tate, Lenny, Gil, Ned, and Bob chased him—as fast as they could.

"Mom!" Davy said. "Dad! They keep copying me.
Tell them to leave me alone!"

"It's only a phase, Davy," Mom said. "Because you're the oldest, your brothers look up to you."

"When they get old enough," said Dad, "your brothers will have their own interests. Then they won't copy you."

Davy groaned.

Petey, Mike, Stu, Mickey, Carl, Pip, Ralph, Tate, Lenny, Gil, Ned, and Bob groaned, too.

One day when Davy sat down to breakfast, he stretched.
But his brothers did not stretch.

"Odd," Davy thought.

Davy poured a big bowl of Toot Loops.

But Petey wanted oatmeal.

Mike and Stu wanted grits.

Mickey, Carl, Pip, and Ralph
wanted scrambled eggs.

Tate, Lenny, and Gil wanted bagels.

Ned and Bob wanted Creamy Wheat.

"Odd," Davy thought.

Davy went for a bike ride. And not one brother rode along.

"Hooray!" Davy shouted. "I guess that terrible phase is over."

So, he spent the rest of the day alone.

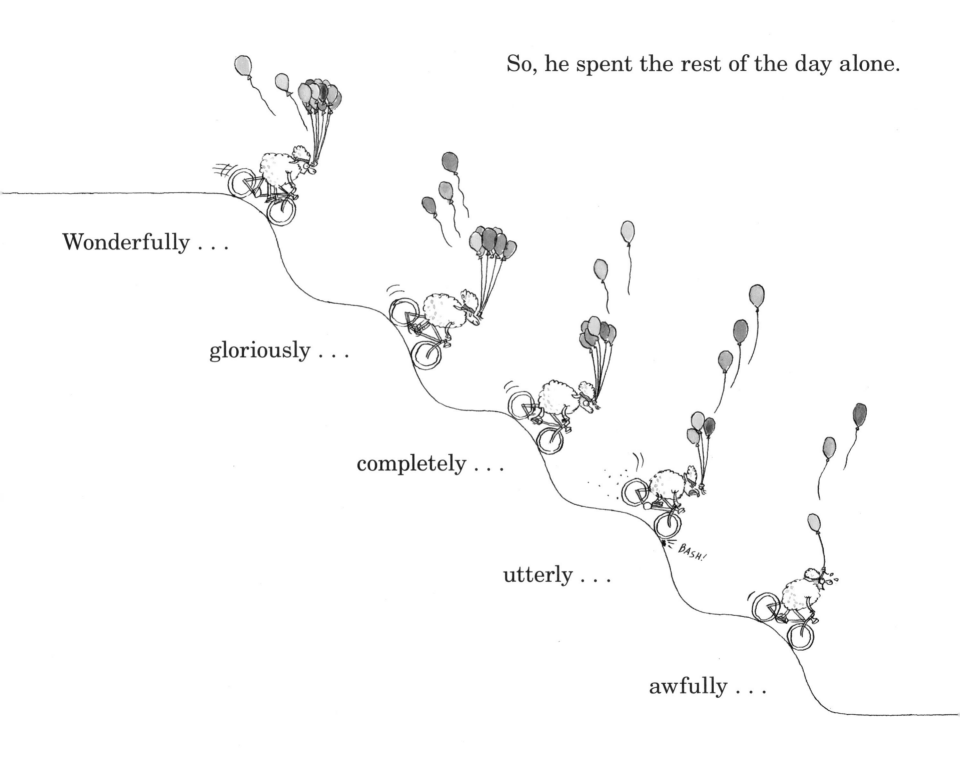

Wonderfully . . .

gloriously . . .

completely . . .

BASH!

utterly . . .

awfully . . .

alone.

Maybe he could play with his brothers.

Petey, Mike, Stu, and Mickey were playing blocks.

But that was for little sheep.

Carl, Pip, Ralph, and Tate were snacking on bananas.
Davy didn't like bananas.

Lenny, Gil, Ned, and Bob were watching *Baby Dude*.
That show gave Davy nightmares.

Not one sheep was left for Davy.
So, he went to bed.

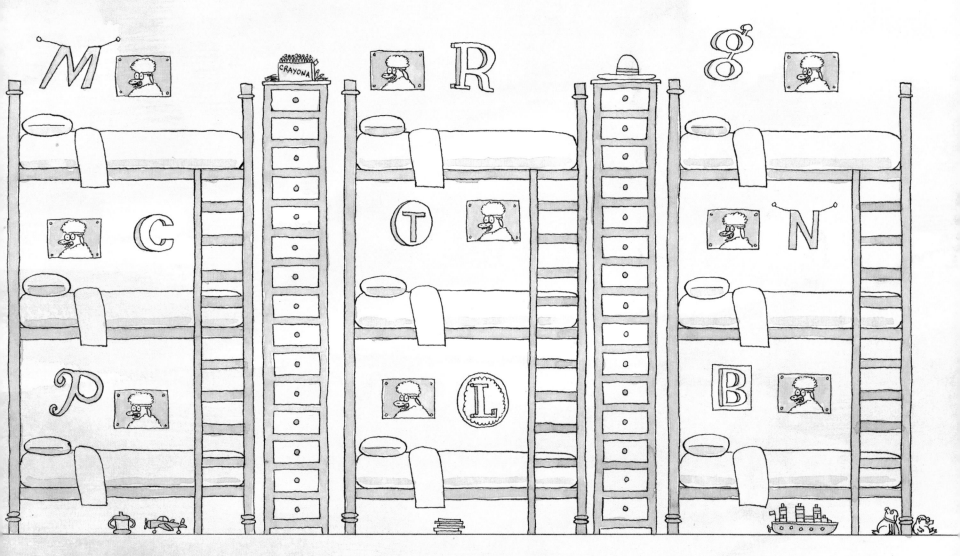

In the morning, Davy yawned a great big yawn.

From the next room came another big yawn.

When he banged his elbow in the bathroom, Davy yelled, "honkin' plunger!"

From the next room came a little voice, "honkin' plunger!"

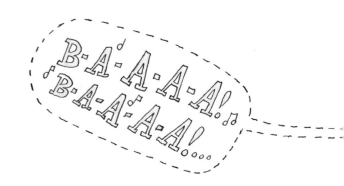

Davy started a song, a tender ballad.
When outside the bathroom came another
voice, singing the same tender ballad.

Could it be . . . another . . .

It was a sister!

And Gertie copied Davy's every move.